Cinderella

FAY'S FAIRY TALES

Cinderella

William Wegman

with Carole Kismaric and Marvin Heiferman

Hyperion
New York

Once upon a time there lived a rich widowed gentleman and his lovely young daughter. Ella, as she was named, was beautiful, adorable, and intelligent. Her father was devoted to her, and she in turn loved him. She caused her father no trouble at all, but for reasons we shall never know, he thought she needed a mother's attention. He began looking for a wife. The woman he chose had two daughters about Ella's age. "Perfect," he thought, "Ella will have a mother to care for her and two sisters as playmates. She will never be sad or bored." All he cared about was Ella. This seemed like a perfect arrangement. Before he could find out otherwise, he died.

It did not take long for the stepmother to reveal her evil nature. Ella quickly learned that a smiling stepmother was not necessarily a good sign. She smiled when she turned Ella out of her room to make a bigger dressing room for her own daughters. She smiled with each new chore and thankless task she thought up for Ella — like beating rugs, scrubbing the kitchen floor, or ironing tablecloths, doilies, and frilly bows. She smiled when she pointed to the attic and said to Ella, "Go to your room. From now on this is where you will sleep." The stepmother doted exclusively on her own daughters, who were already spoiled beyond belief.

One of Ella's many chores was sweeping and cleaning the chimneys and removing the ashes and soot from the fireplaces and the cellar. It was a particularly dirty job but one that Ella carried out cheerfully, for it was not in Ella's nature to complain, nor was she offended by the nicknames inflicted upon her. "Ashcan Ella," said the eldest stepsister. "Cellarella," trumpeted the younger. "Cinderella!" they chimed in unison. And the name stuck.

Ella didn't mind the name, and she didn't mind the extra work. She liked to keep busy, for it kept her mind off sad thoughts. She ironed and sewed and swept and did the dishes — both wash and dry! Once, by accident, she broke a small teacup. Fearing punishment, she buried the pieces in the garden and made a little prayer over it.

One day a letter came by special messenger.

By Invitation of the King
Come One and All to a Gala Ball
At the Grand Palace
The First Day of Next Week

The ball was no ordinary event. It was to be the most spectacular ball in the kingdom and was certainly the most talked about. Everybody knew that the real reason for the ball was to find a bride for the king's son, the very handsome, very eligible young prince.

The stepmother was agitated beyond belief. "Only a few days to prepare," she complained. She pictured herself queen-in-law of the castle. What great rooms would be hers! What jewels she would wear, the most opulent in all the land! There was no question in her mind that the prince would choose one of her own daughters to be his wife. Of that she was certain. The only question was, which one?

The stepsisters were in a tizzy. "Cinders, sweet thing, would you pretty please add an appliqué to my dress?" "Cin, be a love and fetch me a flower from the garden for my corsage." "Ella, could you please hem my blue dress just in case I want to wear it?" Ella was very good at sewing and tying bows and making special decorations for their hair, and the stepsisters relied on her expertise. "What should I wear?" "How should I do my hair?" The youngest stepsister liked yellow because she was heavy and she thought yellow made her look light. The eldest, who had no sense of her own, liked pink because someone had said that pink was feminine and pretty.

Cinderella had hopes of going to the ball, too, but they were dashed by her stepmother. It seemed her ball gown was sent overseas by mistake. At least that was what the stepmother claimed.

All day and into the next, Cinderella helped her sisters dress and redress without complaint. At last the carriage came to pick them up and take them to the ball. As Cinderella watched the coach disappear over the horizon, a thought occurred to her. What if I make my own dress? Then I could go to the ball! Determined to try, she went off to the workroom. There she found some leftover blue satin, nylon netting, red silk, bits of lace, and almost a foot of perfectly good fringe, and with these scraps she managed to piece together a gown. Looking down at her tattered sandals, however, Cinderella realized that without proper shoes she could never go to the ball. Defeated and in great despair, Cinderella slowly climbed the long staircase to her room, where she cried herself to sleep.

She awakened to a glowing light, which she at first mistook for morning. Turning toward the window she saw before her a vision so lovely, radiant, and serene it could only be…

"Cinderella, I am your Fairy Godmother," a sweet voice said. The beautiful fairy waved her magic wand, drawing Cinderella to her. Together they floated down into the garden.

"I am here to grant your wish. I understand you want to go to the ball. First you need a carriage. Go get me a pumpkin. Over there, that nice big fat one." *Zap!* All at once, the pumpkin was transformed into a beautiful golden carriage.

"Goodness gracious!" exclaimed Cinderella.

"Now you will need a debonair footman. Fetch me that charming rat in the basement." Obediently Cinderella returned with the creature and placed it on the ground before the Fairy Godmother, who, with a flick of her wand, transformed the rat into a debonair footman.

"And now, for a fine coachman to drive your coach. Over there...," she said, pointing, "this lizard will do perfectly. Place it upon your fair head."

"Really?" said Cinderella, but she obeyed. *Zap!* The splendid green coachman seemed as amazed by the transformation as was Cinderella.

"And how about those little garden mice you have made friends with?" the Fairy Godmother continued. Cinderella ran to the garden and returned with two handfuls, six mice to be exact. And with six taps of the Fairy God-mother's magic wand they became the most noble, spirited coach horses in all the land.

"Now you are ready for the ball. Except..."

"Except for the way I'm dressed!"

"No problem. Voilà." Then the Fairy Godmother pointed the magic wand at Cinderella and with a simple "ta-da" turned Cinderella's frock into the most beautiful gown in the world, complete with matching corsage and tiara. Cinderella still wore sandals, but, before she could even look down, they became the most beautiful glass slippers that ever were. They were not the kind of glass slippers that could break or could cut you. "Look, they glow!" exclaimed Cinderella.

"Now you are ready to go to the ball, Cinderella, but you must know and respect one thing. You *must* be home by midnight," the Fairy Godmother warned her. "If you are not back at the stroke of twelve, all will become as it once was — the coach will turn back into a pumpkin, your footman will once again be a rat, the coachman a lizard, the six fine horses six mice, and your beautiful gown nothing more than your tattered frock."

"I promise," said Cinderella, and away she went into the night in her stunning coach.

At the castle, the ball was in full swing, and what a glamorous and glitzy event it was! The royal chamber orchestra with its internationally renowned violins played stately courantes and spirited gigues with great sparkle and polish. No expense was spared on the decorations or the food. Excellent hors d'oeuvres were offered continuously.

Meanwhile, the prince was not exactly having the time of his life. Frankly, he was a bit bored, particularly by two sisters who stuck to him like frosting on a cake.

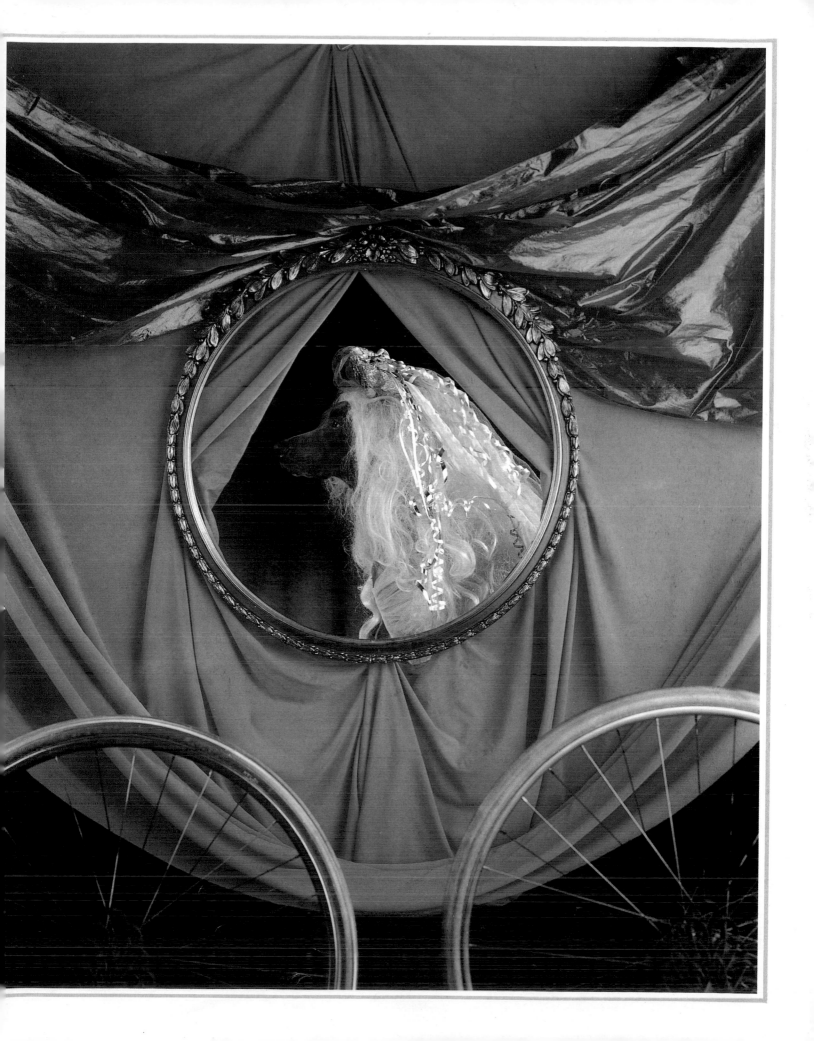

Suddenly a mysterious guest arrived. For a moment the orchestra stopped playing. Everyone stopped dancing. A hush swept the room. "Who is she?" "Who is this exceptional beauty?" "Is she the daughter of a duke?" "Is she a princess from some unknown kingdom?"

"I must know," said the prince, and, politely excusing himself from the next dance, he dashed across the ballroom floor to meet her.

The mysterious guest was so beautiful that the prince found himself unable to talk. He stood there awkwardly, and she startled him by speaking perfect Old French, a language not spoken since the days of the troubadours. She soon regained her normal voice, which was genteel but not so pretentious. His shyness eased, and before long they were dancing. First a gavotte, then a minuet, followed by a most dignified sarabande. Then the daring waltz, all the rage amongst those in the know. Where did she learn to dance this way? It was as if she were transported by her special glass slippers. Dance after dance was theirs. No one dared to interrupt them. Not even her own stepsisters could guess that this mysterious guest was Cinderella. They were beside themselves with jealousy.

Cinderella was so happy that she forgot about the time. Her feet never quite seemed to touch the ground as she danced and danced. Suddenly she remembered the words of her Fairy Godmother. "You *must* be home by midnight." She rushed to the window. "Oh no!" exclaimed Cinderella. The clock in the castle courtyard read 11:59. Inside, the great gilded clock began to strike twelve: *Bong! Bong! Bong!* Cinderella fled in a panic. Across the crowded ballroom floor and through the castle halls she ran. Rounding the corner at the head of the staircase, she tripped, leaving behind one glass slipper.

She hesitated for a moment, but it was too late to turn back. She descended the grand staircase and fled the castle, racing past a lizard, six brown mice, a rat, and a sad looking pumpkin. She ran and ran into the night, her once fine gown disintegrating behind her, and with it her regal tiara and corsage. "Oh dear!" cried Cinderella. At last she reached home, dressed in her humble paisley frock, still holding one glass slipper. No one was there yet. She hid the slipper in the basement, where no one would find it. If only she had heeded the words of her Fairy Godmother. But what an evening! The prince...so handsome, so dashing. How well they danced together. They had only spent a few hours together, yet she would never forget him.

Her reverie was broken by the clatter of the horse-drawn carriage and the unmistakable chatter of her stepsisters. Although tired and bedraggled, they could hardly wait to tell Cinderella all about their extraordinary evening, and especially about how the prince was so smitten, first with one and then the other.

"He couldn't take his eyes off me," bragged the elder. "Did you see the way he looked at me?" said the younger, pretending to blush. "What a wolf!" No mention was made of the mysterious "princess."

Meanwhile back at the palace, the prince was in a state of great distress. His dog, Robare, led the prince to the head of the grand stairway, where he had found the lost glass slipper. The sight of the tiny delicate shoe made the prince dizzy. His heart ached and his head was spinning. Who was she? How will I ever find her? He did not even know her first name. All he had was her glass slipper. He made an oath to find her, a vow to search every household in the kingdom. He would do whatever it took, no matter how long it might take to find her. He would dispatch his own royal emissary, with the slipper carefully placed on a red velvet pillow. The maiden whose foot perfectly fit into the slipper would be his princess.

Day after day the shoe bearer went from house to house in search of the maiden whose foot would fit the slipper. "Under the authority given to me by royal decree of the prince, I hereby command that you try on this slipper." But to no avail.

When the royal shoe bearer arrived at her house, Cinderella was busy sweeping the basement. The stepsisters practically trampled the poor fellow in their efforts to be the first to try on the coveted slipper. The elder thrust her foot at him. It looked huge next to the delicate slipper. The younger followed, extending the wrong foot, not that the correct foot fit any better. The elder tried shrinking her foot by soaking it in ice water, but in vain. The slipper fit only one foot: a slender, delicate one, and that foot belonged to no one, it seemed to the emissary, for he had been everywhere and seen everyone. As he was leaving, he heard a noise in the basement.

"Who's there?" he asked. "Nobody of concern," replied the stepmother. "Only Cinderella," chimed in the stepsisters. "And we know that she did not go to the ball, because we were there, and Cinderella definitely was not. She couldn't go. She had nothing to wear," they said smugly.

"Nevertheless," said the shoe bearer, "I am under oath to the prince that no maiden be overlooked and no fair foot be left untried. Present her!" he demanded.

"Very well," said the stepmother, pointing to the cellar door. "You will find her in the basement. But you're wasting your time." The emissary went down the dark stairs, followed by the mocking stepmother and her two giggling daughters.

Cinderella saw the shoe bearer and stopped sweeping. In spite of her plain dress, he could see that she was lovely.

"Under the authority given to me by royal decree of the prince, I hereby command that you try on this slipper." He presented Cinderella with the glass slipper perched upon a red velvet pillow.

Cinderella came forward and effortlessly slid her foot into the slipper. The slipper began to glow.

The stepsisters were shocked. "What an impossible coincidence!" said the eldest. "Yes, a freak occurrence!" said the youngest. "This is quite impossible!" said the stepmother. All doubt vanished, however, when Cinderella produced the slipper's mate from her basement hiding place. It, too, fit perfectly.

The shoe bearer said urgently, "Cinderella, we must go immediately to the castle."

The stepmother looked pale. She had to sit down. Recovering, she smiled at Cinderella, calling her "Darling" and "Sweetie." She ordered one of the stepsisters to bring Cinderella a cold beverage, "Or perhaps something hot?"

"I must go," said Cinderella to her stepmother, trying not to be rude, and, excusing herself, she went upstairs to gather her meager belongings.

To her surprise, she found in her room a complete wardrobe of lovely clothes, everything from casual to formal. She found nice soaps and shampoos and pretty things for her hair. How happy and excited she was! Cinderella knew that her Fairy Godmother had returned.

Back at the castle, the prince paced and fretted on the balcony. He watched and waited nervously for signs of the emissary's return. Suddenly, off in the distance, he caught sight of the royal carriage, and he knew that the princess had been found at last. He raced through the castle and into the courtyard, arriving just in time to help Cinderella from the carriage. She curtsied demurely, and he bowed to her with great respect. Arm in arm they walked through the castle gates. They gazed into each other's eyes and saw that they were in love.

After a brief engagement, they were married. And what a spectacular wedding it was! Everyone was invited, even Cinderella's stepmother and her two stepsisters, who, after the wedding, moved into the castle where Cinderella and the prince lived happily ever after.

Text and photographs © 1993 by William Wegman.
Printed in the United States of America.
For information address Hyperion Books for Children,
114 Fifth Avenue, New York, New York 10011.
First Edition
7 9 10 8 6

Library of Congress Cataloging-in-Publication Data

Wegman, William.
Cinderella/William Wegman, with Carole Kismaric and Marvin
Heiferman. — 1st ed.
p. cm. — (Fay's fairy tales)
Summary: In her haste to flee the palace before her fairy
godmother's magic loses effect, Cinderella leaves behind a glass
slipper. Photographs show the characters depicted as dogs.
ISBN 1-56282-348-5 (trade) — ISBN 1-56282-349-3 (lib. bdg.)
[1. Fairy tales.] I. Kismaric, Carole. II. Heiferman,
Marvin. III. Title. IV. Series: Wegman, William. Fay's fairy
tales.
PZ8.W424Ci 1993
398.21 — dc20
[E] 92-72028 CIP AC

Acknowledgments

With thanks to
Virginia Alexander, Andrea Beeman, Alison Berry,
Nancy Boas, Judith Bobb, Jason Burch, Christine
Burgin, Lely Constantinople, David Corey, Suzanne
Farrell, Stacy Fischer, Lance Fung, Pamela Gaul, Sharon
and Gregg Hartmann, Suzanne Lipschutz, Susan Litecky,
Pat and Connie O'Brien, John Reuter, Lynda Rodolitz,
Dale Rubin, Steve Rubin, Robert Vissichio,
Jeanette Ward, Pam Wegman,
W.J. Fantasy, and The Pace/MacGill Gallery.

Cinderella
was developed and edited
by William Wegman
with Marvin Heiferman and Carole Kismaric/
Lookout Books, New York.